Table of Contents

Can you find these words?

birds

cats

crickets

goldfish

3

4

cats

6

goldfish

Crickets are popular pets in China.

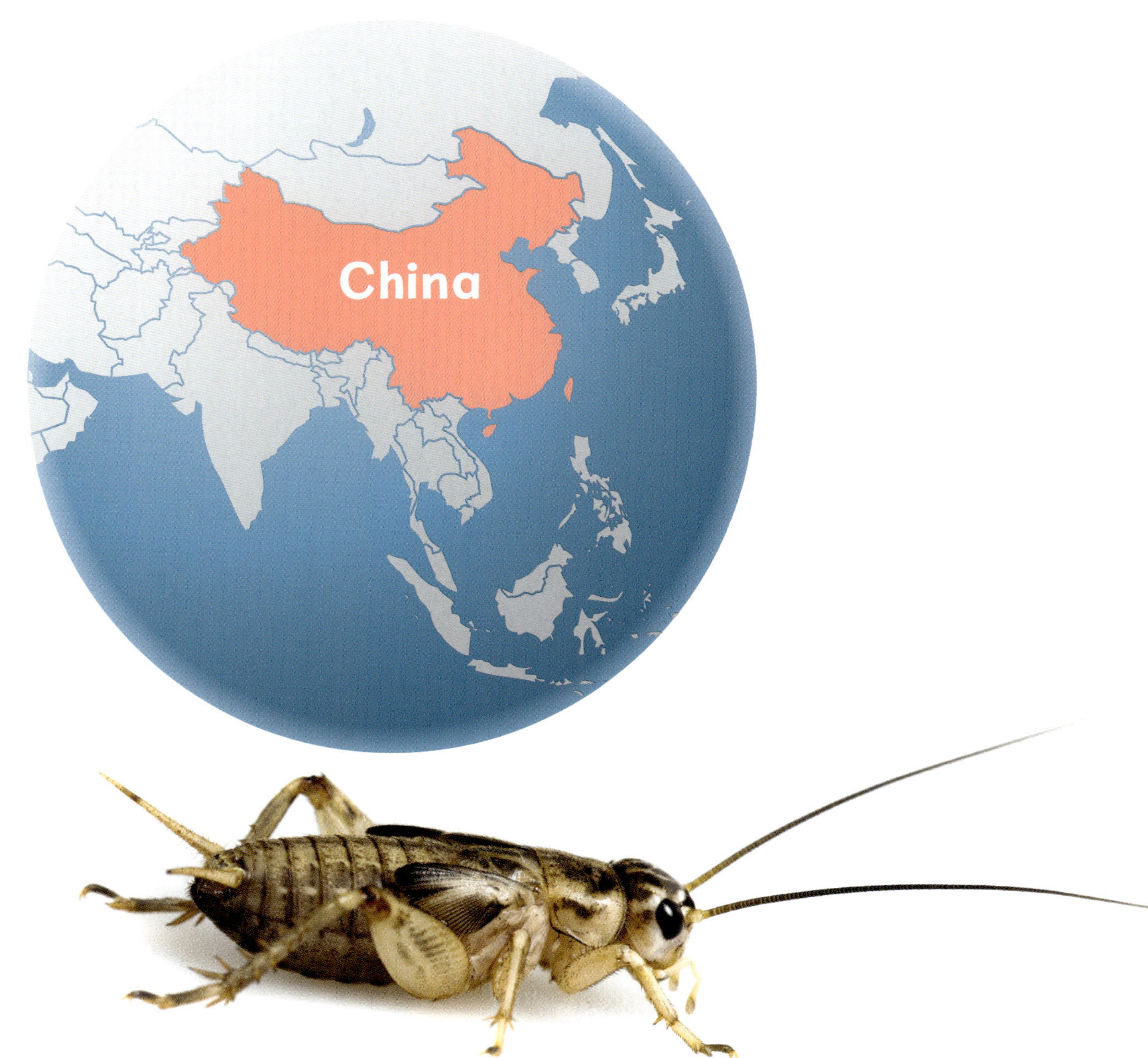

8

9

People in India enjoy these **birds**.
India

They are called budgies.

Dogs are the most popular pet in the world.

Did you find these words?

People in India enjoy these **birds**.

Cats are popular pets in Russia.

Crickets are popular pets in China.

Goldfish are popular pets in Britain.

Photo Glossary

birds (burdz): Animals that have two legs, wings, feathers, and a beak.

cats (kats): Small, furry animals with claws and whiskers, often kept as pets.

crickets (KRIK-itz): Insects that jump and make chirping sounds.

goldfish (GOHLD-fish): A reddish-gold fish that can be seen in ponds and aquariums.

About the Author

Katy Duffield is an author who has had LOTS of pets. She's had cats, dogs, fish, horses, crabs, birds, turtles, lizards, gerbils, and many others. Right now, she has one pet—her sweet and funny dog, Pedro.

www.rourkebooks.com

PHOTO CREDITS: Cover: ©Sergii Figurnyi; p.2,10-11,14,15: ©Africa Studio; p.2,4-5,14,15: ©Oleksandr Lytvynenko; p.2,8-9,14,15: ©Kuttelvaserova Stuchelova; p.2,6-7,14,15: ©satit_srihin; p.3: ©Serafima; p.12-13: ©andresr

Edited by: Keli Sipperley
Cover and Interior design by: Rhea Magaro-Wallace

Library of Congress PCN Data
Pets Around the World / Katy Duffield
(Time to Discover)
ISBN (hard cover)(alk. paper) 978-1-64156-207-2
ISBN (soft cover) 978-1-64156-263-8
ISBN (e-Book) 978-1-64156-311-6
Library of Congress Control Number: 2017957905

Printed in the United States of America
02-3532211937